TIME★TWISTERS

AMELIA EARHART AND THE FLYING CHARIOT

ALSO BY STEVE SHEINKIN

TIME★TWISTERS

AMELIA EARHART AND THE FLYING CHARIOT

STEVE SHEINKIN

ROARING BROOK PRESS

New York

Text copyright © 2019 by Steve Sheinkin

Illustrations copyright © 2019 by Neil Swaab

Published by Roaring Brook Press

Roaring Brook Press is a division of Holtzbrinck Publishing Holdings Limited Partnership

175 Fifth Avenue, New York, NY 10010

mackids.com

Library of Congress Control Number: 2018944867

Paperback ISBN: 978-1-250-15257-2

Hardcover ISBN: 978-1-250-14899-5

Our books may be purchased in bulk for promotional, educational, or business use. Please contact your local bookseller or the Macmillan Corporate and Premium Sales Department at (800) 221-7945 ext. 5442 or by email at MacmillanSpecialMarkets@macmillan.com.

First edition, 2019

Book design by Neil Swaab

Printed in the United States of America by LSC Communications, Harrisonburg, Virginia

Paperback: 10 9 8 7 6 5 4 3 2 1

Hardcover: 10 9 8 7 6 5 4 3 2 1

For Anna—your Amelia Earhart Halloween costume helped inspire this book!

CHAPTER ONE

The bell rang. The kids cheered.

"Okay, guys," Ms. Maybee told her fourth-grade class, "see you Monday!"

Everyone got up and started shoving stuff into backpacks. Except for Abby and Doc. They stayed slumped in their chairs.

ABBY.
SHE ONCE HELPED NEIL ARMSTRONG LAND ON THE MOON.

DOC.
HE WAS ONCE A LOOKOUT ON A PIRATE SHIP. (HE WASN'T VERY GOOD.)

Between school, soccer, and fixing history, it had been a tiring week.

Ms. Maybee walked up to them. "I know I'm fascinating, but you really do have to leave."

Abby yawned. Doc nodded sleepily.

They stumbled toward the library, eyes half closed. They shuffled past the checkout desk.

"Abby and Doc! The ones who broke history!"

That woke them up a bit. They turned to see who'd spoken.

It was a girl. About nine, their age. She stood in front of the librarian's bulletin board, which was filled with photos of students in their Halloween costumes.

Hi, I'm Sarah, but everyone calls me Sally.

the girl said, speaking in quick bursts.

"I'm homeschooled, but they let me use the library. I've heard about the strange things that have been happening. Abe Lincoln becoming a pro wrestler! Abigail Adams on a pirate ship! It *was* you, right? The ones who broke history?"

"It was really more Lincoln's fault," Doc said.

"That's what I heard," Sally said.

"We've been trying to fix things," Abby said.

"Must be fun!" Sally shouted.

Abby and Doc looked at each other. They weren't sure if they were supposed to talk about this. And anyway, they didn't have the energy to explain.

"Well, it was nice to meet you," Abby said.

"Yeah," Doc said. "See you."

They trudged between tall shelves to the back of the library.

Sally followed. "Where are you going

now? The Wild West? King Arthur's Court?"

"We're going to wait for our mom," Doc said.

"Oh."

They stopped in front of the door to the storage room.

"She's a teacher here," Abby said. "We sit back in this storage room after school, do homework and stuff, till she's ready to leave."

Sally smiled. "Well, guess I'll get back to my reading. See you later?"

"Yeah," Doc said, yawning. "Sure."

Abby and Doc went into the storage room and shut the door. The small space had bookshelves, a table, two chairs, and a tall cardboard box that somehow took Abby and Doc to times and places they read about in history class.

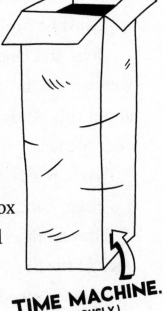

TIME MACHINE.
(SERIOUSLY.)

People from history could use the box, too. That's how all the trouble began. Abraham Lincoln had jumped out of the box and announced he was quitting history—and became a pro wrestler instead. Doc and Abby convinced him to go back to being president of the United States. But other people from history saw what Lincoln had done. If Lincoln could travel through time, so could they. Abigail Adams, the first lady, joined a pirate ship. The cowboy Nat Love flew to the moon.

Getting everyone back where they belonged was exhausting. All Doc and Abby wanted to do now was rest.

They threw down their backpacks and fell into the chairs. Abby took off her glasses, folded her arms on the table, and rested her head in her arms. Doc put his feet up on the table and tilted his head back. His baseball hat dropped to the floor.

They both closed their eyes, hoping for a nice long nap.

Which they would not get.

CHAPTER TWO

"**W**ake up, sleepyheads! Time to go home!"
Doc's chair tipped back, and he crashed to the floor.

"Whaaaa?" Abby groaned, wiping drool from her mouth. "Oh, hi, Mom."

Their mom stood in the doorway. She laughed.

"It's Friday," said Doc, lying flat on his back. "No homework."

Abby reached for her glasses.

They weren't there.

Instead, right where she'd left the glasses was a pair of goggles.

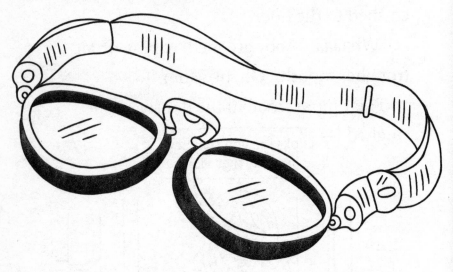

"What?" Abby asked. "Where are my glasses?"

"And my hat," Doc said, looking around. "Where's my hat?"

"Abigail," their mom said, "*please* tell me you did not lose your glasses."

"I didn't!"

"Where are they?"

"I don't know."

"That's the definition of *lost*, last I checked." Their mom sighed. "Do you still have that old pair in your bag?"

"I hate those," Abby moaned.

"Just till you find your good ones. Get your stuff together, both of you, and meet me in my classroom."

Abby reached into a pocket in her backpack and pulled out the glasses she'd gotten in kindergarten. They had goofy tiger-stripe frames. She put them on.

Abby picked up the goggles. They looked like the kind pilots wore in the early days of airplanes. They sort of reminded her of Amelia Earhart's flight goggles.

Abby was a big fan of Amelia Earhart, the famous pilot. She'd been Amelia for Halloween, and her costume had come with goggles just like these. But those were cheap plastic. These were much heavier, with glass lenses and metal frames.

She put the goggles on over her glasses. The canvas strap was loose, as if it had been adjusted to fit a bigger head.

"Look at this," Doc said, touching the back of the strap. On the strap, in black ink, were two letters:

AE

"That's how Amelia Earhart signed letters: *AE*," Abby said.

"Could they be real?" Doc wondered. "Really Amelia's?"

"Things *have* been getting mixed up lately," Abby pointed out.

"Yeah, but mostly people from history. Not, you know, eyewear."

They both looked at the tall cardboard box.

Abby walked to the box. She tilted it toward her and looked in.

"No glasses in here," Abby said.

"How about my hat?"

"Just a few history books at the bottom. Same as always."

Abby stepped onto a chair, then up onto the table. From there, she stepped up to the top of a wobbly stack of boxes. She tightened the strap on the pilot goggles.

"Mind if I ask what you're doing?" Doc said.

"I need to give these back," Abby said,

tapping the goggles. "And see if she has my glasses."

"Why would Amelia Earhart have your glasses?" Doc asked.

"I don't know, but Mom's gonna be mad if I can't find them," Abby said. "Plus, I always wanted to meet her."

"I don't think that's what the cardboard box is for."

"Okay, box," Abby said. "I'm not sure exactly where Amelia Earhart is right now, but hopefully you know, so um . . . yeah, thanks."

She bent her knees and jumped toward the tall box. She flew in feet first—and disappeared without a sound.

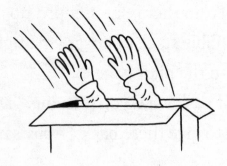

CHAPTER THREE

Abby landed on a concrete floor. She was in a massive building with high ceilings. The air smelled of motor oil and rubber. Small planes were parked all around.

Doc tumbled down a few seconds later. Abby helped him up, and they looked around.

"Airplane hangar," she said.

"And the planes are old," he said.

I mean, old to us.

Abby noticed a calendar hanging on the wall. She ran over to take a look.

It was a calendar from the year 1932. Opened to the page for May.

"We're in 1932," Abby said.

"You gotta love that cardboard box," Doc said.

"May 1932," Abby said. "That's when Amelia Earhart flew solo across the Atlantic. No woman had ever done it before. But I don't see her."

"Let's look outside," Doc suggested.

It was a chilly spring day. There were other hangars and a runway, and trees and fields all around. Above the trees, in the distance, they could see the top of New York City's Empire State Building. Finished just the year before, it was the tallest building in the world.

"We're in New Jersey," Abby said. "Teterboro Airport. I read about this. This is where Amelia got ready for her Atlantic flight. Look!"

Abby pointed to Amelia Earhart's famous

Lockheed Vega. She'd seen the airplane a hundred times in photos—black-and-white photos. In person, it was fire-engine red.

Amelia Earhart stood near the small plane, talking to newspaper reporters. She wore long pants and a leather jacket. Her short, wavy hair flapped in the breeze.

No goggles.

That's a great question. I'm glad you asked it!

Abby and Doc walked up and stood behind the reporters.

"Women, like men, should try to do the impossible," Amelia was telling them. "And when they fail? Their failure should be a challenge to others."

"But aren't you worried?" one of the reporters asked. "Failure in this case . . . that is, over the Atlantic Ocean. Not much room for error, is there?"

"The thing is to decide if a goal is worth the risks involved," Amelia said. "If it is, stop worrying and try." She looked up at the sky. "All I need now is a good weather report."

"Any last message to our readers?" asked another reporter. "I'm sorry, not *last* message. Just, last for now . . ."

Amelia laughed. "I don't claim to be the bravest pilot, and I'm certainly not the best. But my motto is:

"Thanks. Can we get a few pictures?"

"Certainly."

When the photographers were finished, Abby stepped forward. She was still wearing the goggles.

She said, "Ms. Earhart, I—*owwww!*"

A tall man in a suit had just grabbed her by the back of the neck.

"Caught ya!" the man barked.

Doc shouted, "Hey, let go of her!"

The man grabbed Doc, too, and dragged them both toward the nearest hangar.

"Here's a story for you," he called to the newspapermen. "Make a swell headline: AMELIA EARHART GOGGLE THIEVES NABBED AT AIRPORT!"

CHAPTER FOUR

The man was George Putnam, Amelia Earhart's manager—and husband. He shoved Abby and Doc into an office in the hangar and glared down at them.

I **thought** I saw someone sneaking around here.

"It wasn't me!" Abby insisted.

"It *wasn't*," Doc said. "We just got here."

"It was both of you," Putnam charged. He snatched the goggles from Abby's face.

"I didn't steal them!"

"Sure, sure," Putnam said. "They just happened to appear on your head."

"Funny," Doc said, "but that's kind of close."

"Can we at least talk to her?" Abby asked.

"To Amelia? You most certainly cannot." Putnam picked up a phone. "Ever since she became famous, people have been stealing things from her—goggles, scarves, maps, you name it. Do you know, people steal things and then bring them to her to autograph? The nerve! We're sick of it!" And he growled into the phone, "Yes, operator. Get me the police."

"But we didn't take anything!" Abby repeated. "Actually, I think *she* might have something of *mine*."

"Tell it to the judge," Putnam said.

A voice from the other side of the door called out. "Hold on there, GP!"

"Yes, I'm still waiting," Putnam said into the phone. "Hello? Hello? Officer?"

Amelia Earhart walked into the office.

"What did you say?" she asked Abby. "You think I have something of yours?"

Abby looked up at Amelia. She felt a blush spread over her cheeks. She opened her mouth, but no sound came out.

Gasp.

Doc came to the rescue. "This is my sister, Abby. I'm Doc. You're her hero."

"How flattering."

"One of them, anyway," Doc added.

"Hang up the phone, GP," Amelia said. "Go see if Brent has anything new on the weather."

"Fine," Putnam grunted, tossing the goggles onto the desk. "But don't waste too much time with these kids."

He stomped out. Amelia picked up the goggles.

"These are mine all right," she said. "Where on earth did you find them?"

Abby explained. Amelia didn't seem surprised.

"I've heard things have gotten a little twisted up lately," she said. "I suppose you're hoping I have your glasses?"

Abby nodded.

"And my hat," Doc said. "Red baseball hat?"

"Follow me," Amelia said.

She led them out of the office and across

the hangar to a wall where hats, coats, and small bags hung from hooks.

"I left my goggles in this bag yesterday," Amelia said. "And this morning, they weren't there." She reached into her bag. "But *this* was."

She pulled out—not Abby's glasses.

Not Doc's hat.

Some sort of stick? No, a small wreath. A leafy branch tied in a circle, about the size of a crown.

Everyone was pretty confused.

"Can I see?" Doc asked.

Amelia handed Doc the wreath.

"Kind of looks like an olive branch," he said. "They used to give crowns like this to winners at the Olympics. Way back in ancient Greece."

Doc put the wreath on his head. "I was an ancient Olympic champion for Halloween," he explained to Amelia Earhart.

Abby rolled her eyes. "I remember you went on and on about how the athletes did the events totally naked."

"Kids loved it!" Doc said. "Grown-ups just want to tell you the boring parts of history."

George Putnam came running up. "Amelia! There you are!"

"What is it?" Amelia asked. "Is everything all right?"

"Super!" Putnam shouted. "Just heard from the weather bureau. Expecting calm skies over the Atlantic for the next two days."

"Finally!" Amelia shouted.

She reached into her bag and pulled out her leather flying helmet. She put it on and strapped the goggles over the helmet, resting the frames on her forehead. Then she turned to Abby and Doc.

"Thank you again," she said, tapping the goggles. "I'm sorry about your glasses, Abby. I hope they turn up. Well, wish me luck!"

And she raced out to her plane.

CHAPTER FIVE

Abby and Doc were left standing in the hangar.

"No one seems too worried about my hat," Doc said.

Abby barely heard him. She was still a little in shock. "I can't believe I got to meet Amelia Earhart..."

"Weird, about this thing," Doc said, taking the olive branch crown off his head.

"Huh?" Abby asked. "Oh, yeah. Weird."

"You were Amelia Earhart for Halloween," Doc said. "And I was an Olympic athlete. And we find Amelia Earhart's goggles and this thing that looks like an Olympic crown."

"It's a weird coincidence," Abby said.

"Yeah," Doc said. "Or something."

He felt the leaves of the crown. He sniffed the wood. "It's a real branch. Not like the fake one in my costume. And I had to wear that stupid robe-type thing, which was so unrealistic."

"Well, Dad was right not to let you go trick-or-treating naked."

"I guess," Doc said. "It *was* a chilly night."

"What does all this have to do with my glasses?" Abby wondered.

"Remember when I was with the cowboys in Texas, before you got there?" Doc asked. "Abe Lincoln told me he thinks someone's messing with history. Purposely mixing things up."

"Who?" Abby asked. "Why?"

"He doesn't know."

"Let's figure it out," Abby said. "We need to stick with Amelia Earhart. Come on!"

Abby ran out of the hangar, with Doc close behind.

Amelia was out at her plane, making her pre-flight checks.

"Sorry, children, I can't talk now."

"Can we come?" Abby blurted out.

Amelia ran her hand along the back of the wing. She smiled, taking Abby's question as a joke. "This is a solo flight. That's the whole point."

"But you're not crossing the Atlantic *today*," Abby said. "Your plan is to fly to Canada, so you can leave tomorrow from Newfoundland, which is closer to Europe."

AMELIA'S SOLO TRANSATLANTIC FLIGHT

Canada

United States of America

Newfoundland

Ireland

United Kingdom

ATLANTIC OCEAN

Amelia was impressed. "You know a lot about this."

"Please," Abby said. "We'll just ride with you to Canada."

"I don't know . . ."

"What was it you told that reporter?" Abby said. "You should never turn down an adventure?"

That made Amelia smile. "You understand, I can't bring you back here."

"That's okay," Abby said. "We'll find our own way home."

———•———

Ten minutes later they were in the air.

Doc and Abby sat on a tiny bench behind the cockpit. The cabin was big enough for six seats, but the seats had been removed and replaced with extra fuel tanks for Amelia's historic flight. There are no gas stations in the Atlantic Ocean.

A little window gave them an amazing view of New York City and the Hudson River. The buildings and buses and cars looked like pieces of a board game.

"I never get tired of this!" Amelia said, shouting over the roar of the propeller. "When I was your age, I was drawn to thrilling things: bicycles, horses, fast sleds. Everyone told me to be more ladylike. But why go through a gate, if you can jump over it?"

The plane climbed through a layer of clouds, bouncing like a roller coaster. Doc and Abby gripped the side of the bench.

Amelia turned to them and smiled. "Don't worry, I've been flying for ten years!"

"Is it true that no one wanted to teach you at first?" Abby asked.

"There's this silly idea that women can't handle the pressure of flying! But there were a few women pilots out there, and I found one who would teach me. I was working in an office back then, filing, sorting mail; it was awful! But I saved every penny for my lessons. I had no thought of becoming famous. I just lived for this moment—the freedom of the air!"

Doc looked out the window. The clouds were gone now, and he could see straight down, giving him a spectacular view of . . .

"Huh?" he said, elbowing Abby and pointing.

Abby said, "Ms. Earhart?"

"Call me Amelia, please."

"Amelia," Abby said. "I think we made a wrong turn."

CHAPTER SIX

Amelia Earhart's red plane soared above a blue-green sea. The water glittered in bright sunlight and was dotted with small rocky islands. Far in the distance, small waves washed against a white beach.

Amelia leaned to her left and looked down.

That is not New York.

"New Jersey?" Doc asked.

"Not a part I've ever seen," said Amelia. "Looks more like . . . the Mediterranean?"

"Uh-oh," Abby said.

"Yeah," agreed Doc.

Amelia turned to face them. "Do you two know what's going on?"

"No," Abby said. "But this is like what happened to the astronauts. Neil Armstrong and Buzz Aldrin—they were going to the moon, but they suddenly landed in Texas."

"In the 1800s," Doc added. "There were angry cowboys."

"How very inconvenient," Amelia said.

"We wound up fixing everything," Abby said. "Sort of."

Amelia Earhart shook her head. "I really *must* get to Newfoundland tonight. I'm not the only woman who wants to be first across the Atlantic, you know. Another delay, and someone's sure to beat me."

"We'll help you," Doc said.

"And how do you propose to do that?" Amelia snapped. Then she sighed. "I'm sorry, children. I know this is not your fault."

It wasn't. Was it?

Amelia flew toward the land.

"First things first," she said. "Let's figure out where we are."

They sailed over the coast, above rocky hills and forests of pine trees. A few minutes later they spotted a clearing, an area of flat land between green slopes. There were white marble buildings with tall columns and dirt paths between the buildings.

And two large fields. They looked like stadiums. One was empty, but the other was packed with thousands of people.

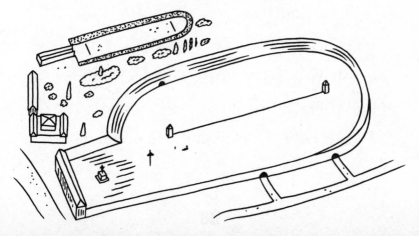

"It looks like Olympia," Doc said. "I mean, I've only seen pictures."

"Olympia?" Abby asked. "Where the Greek gods lived?"

"That's Mount Olympus," Doc explained. "Olympia is different. The site of the ancient Olympics."

"Uh-oh," Abby said again.

There really *was* some kind of competition going on in the stadium. Athletes stood at one end of the field. One of them ran forward with a long spear in his hand. He heaved it high into the air, and it sailed down the field and stuck point first into the reddish-brown dirt. A man in a purple robe ran out to mark the spot. The fans stood and cheered.

"The javelin throw," Doc said.

"Excuse me," Amelia Earhart said. "But are you telling me that's the ancient Olympics down there?"

"Looks like it," Doc said. He pressed his

face against the window. "And the athletes *do* appear to be naked."

Abby cringed. "Why was *that* a good idea?"

Doc laughed. "Supposedly they wore loincloths at first. But then this one guy tripped on his in a race, so he got rid of it. And he won!"

Amelia dove lower for a closer look.

Fans heard the buzz of the engine and looked up, pointing. The only person who didn't notice the strange thing in the sky was the next javelin thrower—his eyes were closed, focused on the toss he was about to attempt.

CENSORED: TOO HOT FOR HISTORY!

With a grunt, he burst forward and threw his spear. The spear soared in a sky-high arc and—

"Look out!" Doc cried. "Javelin!"

—hit the side of the plane with a

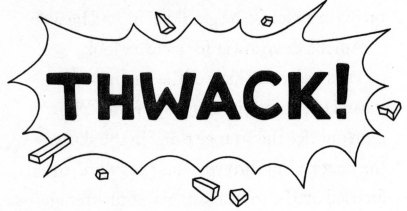

THWACK!

Doc and Abby looked up.

The javelin had pierced the side of the plane, right above their heads. Doc touched the pointed tip with his finger.

That was close.

Amelia turned to look. "Easily fixed," she said calmly. "It's just wood."

"Wood?!" Doc asked. "This plane is made of *wood*?"

"They all were back then," Abby said.

"You were going to cross the Atlantic in a wooden plane?"

"I still am, Doc. Hopefully," Amelia said. "Right now, I better find somewhere to land."

She circled a few hundred feet above Olympia. The grassy areas around the stadium were crowded with people and tents. The only open space was in the second arena—a huge dirt field surrounded by gently sloping hills.

"It's the hippodrome," Doc said. "The field for the chariot races."

"That's our spot!" Amelia said.

CHAPTER SEVEN

A young woman with long black hair stood in the hippodrome. Shielding her eyes with her hand, she looked up at the bright sky.

The woman was Kyniska, a Spartan princess and the owner and trainer of one of the teams in the upcoming chariot race. She'd come to the hippodrome to get in one last workout with her driver and four-horse team.

She watched the red airplane make a slow turn and come in for a landing. Out on the track, her horses trotted along, pulling the chariot and driver—their backs to the approaching plane.

"Talos!" Kyniska shouted. "Get out of the way!"

The driver turned his head and was
startled to see that a flying machine with
a spear in its side was about to land on
him. Screaming, he yanked the reins, and
the horses swerved, tossing him out of the
chariot.

The plane landed, bounced, and rolled to a
stop in a cloud of dust.

The propeller slowed and stopped. The
cockpit window slid open. Amelia Earhart
stuck her head out.

Kyniska ran to her driver. Amelia, Abby, and
Doc jumped out of the plane and rushed over.

Talos was on the ground in a ball, holding his leg. Kyniska and Amelia kneeled beside him.

"My knee . . ." Talos groaned.

"May I check?" Amelia asked. "I was trained as an aide at a military hospital in Canada during the Great War."

Kyniska glared at Amelia Earhart.

"They didn't call it World War I back then," Abby explained. "No one knew there was going to be a second one."

"Who cares about that?" Kyniska snarled, eyes burning with fury. "This is my driver—the best driver in Greece! The race is *tomorrow*!"

———•———

Abby and Doc backed away. Kyniska was still yelling at Amelia Earhart.

"That lady seems pretty upset," Abby said.

"Should we stay with Amelia?" Doc wondered. "Try to help?"

"How?" Abby asked. "The only way to help is to figure out what's going on."

"Agreed."

They ran up the grassy slope surrounding the hippodrome. Doc still had the olive branch crown in his hand.

They looked around. Thousands of fans were streaming out of the stadium, talking and laughing. Vendors pushed carts through the crowds selling grilled meat, bread, and wine. Artists selling sculptures and paintings competed for attention with musicians, dancers, jugglers, and actors.

Bread! Hot and fresh!

And there was the smell.

Abby sniffed the air. Pine forests and wood smoke—that was the good part. But there was more.

"Garbage rotting in the heat," Doc explained. "And body odor. There's not really anywhere to bathe. Plus, they use the dry riverbeds as the bathroom."

"Doc, is everything you know about the Olympics disgusting?"

"That *is* my specialty," Doc said. "But I know other stuff. See those guys?"

He pointed to a group of bearded men in long purple robes.

"Those are the official judges," Doc said. "Maybe they'll know something."

He held up the olive crown.

"Hold on," Abby said. "They're gonna think we stole it."

"No, we can explain," Doc said. Waving the crown in the air, he shouted, "You guys missing one of these?"

The judges stared at the waving crown.

"We didn't steal this!" Doc explained. "It just sort of appeared in a bag belonging to this famous pilot!"

"The stolen crown!" one of them shouted.

"Grab that thief!" shouted another.

"Told you," Abby said.

"It was worth a shot," Doc said, shrugging.

The judges started shoving their way through the crowd toward Doc and Abby.

"Seize those dogs!" a judge roared.

"Should we run?" Abby asked.

Doc nodded. "Run!"

CHAPTER EIGHT

But it wasn't so easy to run. The field was packed with fans and vendors and performers.

Abby tripped over a pile of firewood. Doc slammed into a sword-swallower just as the man was about to lower the blade into his gaping mouth.

Abby scrambled to her feet. Doc picked up the sword he'd knocked from the sword-swallower's hand.

"So what's the trick?" Doc asked the performer. "Do you actually put the whole—"

"Not now, Doc!" Abby yelled.

"Right," Doc said, handing back the sword. "Careful with this."

They took off again, swerving around tents, leaping over campfires. Doc glanced over his shoulder but couldn't see the judges through the crowd.

"Are they chasing us?" Abby asked.

"I'll find out!" Doc said.

Beside him, an actor was standing on a box, reciting a passage from the *Odyssey* in a loud and dramatic voice: "When young rosy-fingered dawn shone once again, the Cyclops lit his fire and—excuse me, young man!"

Doc had just jumped onto the box with the actor.

"Sorry," Doc said. "I just need to . . ."

From that height, he could see the judges. They were definitely chasing, clearing their path by knocking over a vendor's cart, sending fruit flying.

"They're getting closer!" Doc said.

"Where do we go?" Abby asked.

A tent flap opened, and a girl's voice whispered,

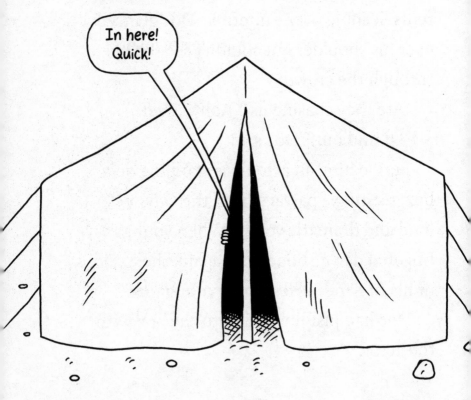

No time to ask questions—Abby and Doc
dove into the tent. The girl crawled outside.

Abby and Doc huddled on the dirt, panting
as quietly as they could, listening to the
action outside.

The actor continued his performance.
"The Cyclops lit his fire and snatched up two
more men for his morning's meal, and then—
hey, get off my box!"

"Get off yourself! We're looking for two
thieves!"

That sounded like one of the judges.

"They've stolen a branch from the sacred
grove of Zeus's temple!" another judge
howled. "They must be thrown off Mount
Kronos!"

"Fine by me," the actor said.

Then a girl's voice shouted: "There they go! Heading toward the hills!"

"Toward the hills!" a judge shouted.

"The hills!" the others called.

The actor cleared his throat and resumed. "And then the monster rolled aside the boulder from the opening of the cave . . ."

The tent flaps opened, and the girl crawled back in.

"They're gone," she said.

"Thanks," Abby said.

"Say nothing of it, my friends."

The girl was wearing robes, like everyone else in Olympia. But she looked familiar to Doc and Abby.

They'd definitely seen her somewhere. Very recently . . .

"Um . . ." Abby said. "Sally?"

Yep, it was Sally—the girl from the library—with a huge grin on her face.

Surprised?

"Very," Abby said. "What are you doing here?"

"I was jealous!" Sally said. "It just seemed so fun!"

"But how'd you get here?" Doc asked. "You know about the, um . . . the cardboard . . ."

Sally laughed. "I've always *adored* the ancient Olympics. I've read stacks of books about the games. So how could I resist! You know, the Olympics were so important to the

Greeks they called a truce. Enemy cities were always fighting one another, but they actually stopped wars for a few weeks so athletes and fans could travel here safely. It all started when the ruler of Elis asked advice from the oracle of Delphi and—"

"Sally, that's very interesting," Abby cut in. "But Amelia Earhart is supposed to take off for Europe very soon."

"From Canada," Doc pointed out. "In 1932."

"We need to get her back there," Abby said. "And we need to figure out who's twisting things up. Stop it from happening again."

"And if we could find my hat," Doc said, "that would be awesome."

Sally nodded. "Okay, I'll help."

"You shouldn't even be here," Doc said.

Sally looked hurt. "It's lonely at home. I don't have many friends."

"Sorry," Doc said. "We're glad you came. We're lucky you did."

"So what now?" Abby wondered. "We can't go out there. Especially you, Doc—the judges got a good look at you."

Doc asked, "Do they really throw people off mountains?"

"Let's not find out," Abby suggested.

"I have an idea," Sally said. "Wait here."

CHAPTER NINE

In the hippodrome, Kyniska sat in the cockpit of Amelia Earhart's plane. She grabbed the control stick, shoving it left and right, forward and back.

"Gently, please!" Amelia pleaded. She was crouching behind Kyniska. "It's the stick. You use it to move the plane up and down. Pushing it forward causes the nose to dip, and you pull it back to climb."

Kyniska yanked it back. "It's not working."

"It also tips the wings," Amelia explained. "The pedals work the rudder."

Kyniska rested her sandals on the pedals.

"You use your feet to move the nose left and right," Amelia said. "These are your instruments," she said, pointing to the panel of dials. "They show your airspeed, height above the ground, engine temperature, oil pressure—everything you need to know."

"I like it," Kyniska said. "I'll take it."

Amelia laughed.

Kyniska wasn't joking.

"But, I . . ." Amelia began. "It's mine. I bought it."

"Yes, and for some reason you chose to crash it into my chariot driver. Do you have any idea how long we have been training for this race?"

"Sorry. How long?"

"Years," Kyniska said. "No woman has ever won an Olympic event. None has ever dared to compete! But I, Kyniska, Princess of Sparta—I am going to be the first winner!"

"But wasn't that other fellow going to drive?" Amelia asked.

"What of it?" Kyniska sneered. "Everyone knows it is the *owner* of the chariot who is considered the champion. It is the owner who wins immortal fame and glory!" She continued in a softer voice. "This has always

been my dream. Since I was a young girl,
I have loved games and sports, any sort of
competition."

"Me too!"

"I bred these horses myself," Kyniska
said. "Trained them, day after day. I have the
greatest team, the finest chariot. I have the
greatest driver—or I did, before you broke his
leg."

"I think it's just a bad bruise," Amelia said.

"He is in no condition to compete."

"No, that's true. How can I make it up to
you?"

"You can't." Kyniska shook her head. "And
so dies my dream, here, on the plains of
Olympia."

They sat in silence.

"What if . . ." Amelia began. "What if I were
to be your driver?"

"*You?*" Kyniska scoffed. "What do you
know of chariot racing?"

"Not much," Amelia admitted. "But I grew up around horses. You could show me."

Kyniska moved the airplane's control stick back and forth. "Well, if you can handle this flying chariot . . ."

"Exactly!" Amelia cried. "It will be an adventure! What could go wrong?"

"Many, many things," Kyniska said, smiling for the first time since she'd met Amelia Earhart. "Come, I will show you!"

CHAPTER TEN

Sally crawled back into the tent. She was holding a fake beard, long and gray, with a string to hold it on.

"When I was walking around before, I noticed a vendor selling these," Sally said. "For women who want to sneak in to watch the events."

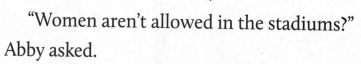

"Women aren't allowed in the stadiums?" Abby asked.

"Nope," Doc said. "Men only. And kids."

"That's lame," Abby said.

"I know," Sally agreed. "Put it on."

"What about me?" Doc asked.

"No one will be able to see you," Sally said. She explained her idea.

Moments later, Sally stood outside the tent. "All clear," she said.

Inside the tent, Abby was wearing the gray beard. Doc shoved the olive wreath into his back pocket. He hunched over, letting his sister climb onto his shoulders. Then, as Doc stood, Abby lifted the corners of the tent and wrapped the canvas around both of them. It looked sort of like a robe.

And it completely covered Doc. Only Abby's bearded head stuck out from the top.

You're heavier than you look.

Quiet.

"Come, father," Sally said. "Let us stroll to the hippodrome."

"Good idea, child," Abby said.

Sally led the way along a path lined with marble statues.

"These are champions of Olympics past," Sally said. "When the games first began, there was only one event, a running race. Over the years, they added jumping, javelin and discus throwing, the chariot race, wrestling, and boxing . . ."

"And it was normal for boxers to get their teeth knocked out," Doc said from inside the tent/robe. "But they didn't like to give their opponents the satisfaction of knowing—so they would swallow their own teeth."

Sally laughed. "I've read that, too!"

"Don't encourage him," Abby said, but with a smile. She liked gross details as much as the next guy.

"Father, look!" Sally said, pointing.

A man in a long purple robe was walking toward them, looking around, clearly searching the crowd.

I know they're here somewhere.

"Judge!" Abby said a little too loudly—to warn Doc, who couldn't see a thing.

"Yes?" the judge said, turning to what appeared to be a wobbly old man. "Did you call me?"

"No, I was just, um . . ." Abby said in a fake deep voice. "How's it going, Your Honor?"

The judge frowned. "We still have not found the wreath thieves."

Doc reached around to his back pocket to make sure the wreath was still there. It was. But when he took his hand off Abby's leg, she tilted forward, nearly sliding off his shoulders, only catching herself by clamping her feet tight to his ribs.

"*Owwww!*" Doc moaned.

The judge looked at Abby.

Abby patted the front of her robe.

"Excuse me," she said. "Too many olives. Well, good luck catching those crooks."

The judge nodded. He turned and continued his search.

"This way, father," Sally said.

They walked on.

"Here's the hippodrome," Sally said.

They looked down at the massive dirt field.

"Six hundred yards long," Sally said. "Two hundred wide."

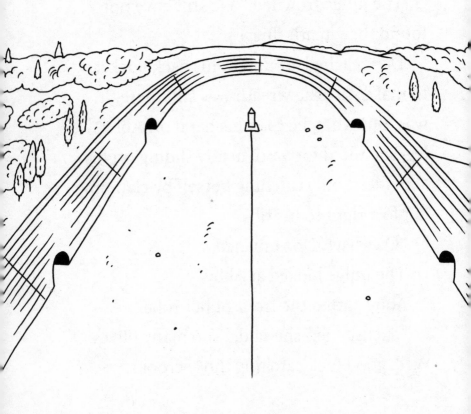

"There's Amelia," Abby said. "And the angry lady. What are they doing?"

Abby's robe opened. Doc peeked out.

Down on the track, Amelia Earhart and Kyniska stood shoulder-to-shoulder in a tiny two-wheeled wooden cart. The chariot bounced along the track, pulled by Kyniska's team of four horses.

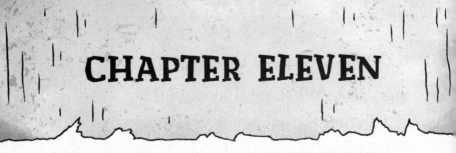

CHAPTER ELEVEN

"**T**his is basically a war chariot," Kyniska explained. "Made to be as light and as fast as possible. They're fragile, easily smashed."

"Kind of like airplanes," Amelia said. She was wearing her flight helmet and goggles.

"Racers may not purposely cause another cart to crash," Kyniska said. "Though it happens all the time. Racers ram each other's chariots. They beat each other with whips. Nothing is done about it."

Careful on the turn!

Amelia pulled the reins, guiding the team around a stone pillar at one end of the arena.

"Turns are the most dangerous part," Kyniska said. "Drivers crash into the post or get tangled in one another's reins and get dragged, trampled."

The chariot swung around the pillar and headed back up the track. There was another pillar at the other end of the field.

"Good, very good," Kyniska said.

"It's a bit like flying," said Amelia.

"You will do well," Kyniska declared. "My horses know what to do. Stay upright, and we will win."

———◆———

Sally, Abby, and Doc walked down the slope to the track. They'd left the tent and beard behind. Doc still had the olive crown in his pocket.

The chariot slowed to a stop. Kyniska and Amelia Earhart hopped out.

"There you are, children," Amelia said.

Abby introduced Sally. Amelia introduced Kyniska.

Sally's eyes lit up. "The first woman to win at the Olympics!"

"That's the plan," Kyniska said.

Sally ran to the chariot and jumped in.

"Careful, child!" Kyniska called.

"I always wanted to try one of these!" Sally yelped. She stood in the chariot, pretending to bounce up and down.

And they're off!

Sally pulls into the lead, blowing past the competition!

Abby turned to Amelia. "Why were *you* driving the chariot?"

"Practicing for the big race tomorrow," Amelia explained.

"You?" Doc asked. "Women can't compete at the ancient Olympics. Can't even watch from the stands."

Amelia tapped her helmet.

"Yeah, but . . ." Abby began. "What about the whole naked thing?"

"Right," Amelia said, suddenly worried. "I hadn't thought of that."

"Chariot racers compete in long robes," Kyniska said. "So drivers are not skinned alive when they fall from their chariots."

"*When* they fall?" Abby asked.

"Well, *if*," Kyniska corrected. "Not everyone is injured. You need not worry, your friend is a natural. What a fine joke it will be on the snooty judges! And best of all is that I cannot lose. If Amelia wins the race, I get the everlasting fame and glory. And if she loses, I get to keep her flying chariot!"

"What? No!" Amelia protested. "I never agreed to that."

Kyniska laughed. "That hardly matters, does it? I have declared it to be so. There is nothing more to discuss."

"I see," Amelia said.

"I guess you have to win," Abby said.

Amelia nodded. "I'll win. But maybe I better get in just one more practice."

She turned to the chariot. Or, to where she'd left it. It wasn't there.

"Look!" Doc shouted, pointing.

Out on the track, Sally stood in Kyniska's chariot, speeding along behind the team of galloping horses.

WHEEEEEE!

"Too fast, child!" Kyniska screamed.

"Whoa!" Sally shrieked, yanking the reins. "How do you stop this thing?"

The chariot raced toward the stone pillar at the far end of the stadium.

Amelia shouted, "Careful on the—"

The horses dashed around the pillar and the chariot swung wide and tipped over and Sally tumbled out.

"—turn!"

CRASH! BANG! BOOM!

Kyniska, Amelia, Abby, and Doc took off
running toward the crash.

Sally sat up and blinked dust from her
eyes.

Pieces of the chariot lay all over the dirt.

CHAPTER TWELVE

Sally stood up. She bent her arms and legs. She hopped up and down. Nothing was broken.

Kyniska got there first, with the others close behind.

"It's all right!" Sally called out. "I'm not hurt!"

Shoving the girl aside, Kyniska bent and picked up a sliver of wood.

My beautiful chariot . . . the finest in Greece . . .

"I'm sorry, Princess," Sally said. "It just looked so fun!"

"First my driver, now my chariot," Kyniska moaned. "What demon of Hades brought you people to Olympia?"

"We're not really sure," Abby said.

"Maybe it can be fixed," Amelia suggested. She looked around at the scattered chariot pieces. There were hundreds. "Maybe not."

Sally looked down at her feet.

Now everyone hates me.

"Come on," Doc said. "We don't hate you."

"I do," Kyniska said, taking an angry step toward Sally.

"Calm down," Abby said. "It was just an accident."

"Thanks, Abby," Sally said, backing away. "But maybe I better head home. See you later?"

"Sure," Doc said. "See you."

Sally turned and ran out of the hippodrome.

Kyniska turned and looked at Amelia Earhart's airplane.

"Well," she said. "At least I get to keep the flying chariot."

———•———

That night, in the hippodrome, Abby, Doc, and Amelia Earhart sat around a campfire.

Abby poked the fire with a long, thin piece of wood—part of the remains of Kyniska's chariot. They'd used other pieces to start the fire.

From the crowded plains above came joyful sounds of laughter and music.

In the hippodrome, no one was laughing.

Doc nibbled a stale cracker. Dinner that night came from a small tin of emergency rations in Amelia's plane.

Amelia stared sadly at her plane. It sat at the edge of the field, guarded by four big-armed men. Kyniska's men.

"She'll take it away in the morning," Amelia said. "I'll never see my Vega again after tonight."

"No, don't say that," Doc said.

"I'm just trying to face the truth. No more Atlantic dreams for me . . ."

"But Ms. Earhart," Abby said. "Amelia. Didn't you fly across the Atlantic once already?"

Amelia nodded, smiling at the memory.

"Yes," she said. "It was the flight that made me famous. Though I hardly deserved the fame."

"Why not?" asked Doc.

"This was back in 1928," Amelia began. "No woman had ever flown over the Atlantic, even as a passenger. It's such a dangerous thing to try. Well, a New York City publisher, George Putnam—"

"Your husband?" Abby asked.

"Not at the time," Amelia said. "I'd never

met him. In any case, he knew a good story
when he saw one. He helped arrange the
flight. I was to fly across the ocean with
two men, a pilot and a navigator. Of course,
I knew they were just using me to get
attention. But what an adventure! Besides, I'd
been a licensed pilot for years and was hoping
to get a chance at the controls.

1928 TRANSATLANTIC FLIGHT CREW

AMELIA EARHART
Passenger / Flight Log

WILMER STULTZ
Pilot

LOUIS GORDON
Copilot / Mechanic

"As it turned out, the weather was lousy the whole way across. I never got a chance to fly. We made it, though. Just over twenty hours to the coast of Britain. And for that—for sitting in the back of a plane like a sack of potatoes—I achieved instant fame!"

Amelia laughed. "I can't complain. I've been making a good living ever since, giving lectures about flying, writing articles, even a book. But I've never been able to shake the feeling that I don't deserve all the praise, all the fame. That's why I am so determined to cross the Atlantic again. This time, alone."

They all sat silently for a while, staring into the fire.

Abby said, "There's got to be *some* way to win that race tomorrow."

"If only there was a chariot we could use," Doc said.

Abby looked over at Amelia's plane. "Maybe there is."

"It's a little heavy," Doc pointed out.

"Better than nothing," Amelia said. "At least I'd have a chance!"

CHAPTER THIRTEEN

The next morning, as the sun rose above the pine hills of Olympia, forty thousand fans streamed into the hippodrome. They packed the grassy slopes surrounding the track.

It was time for the biggest event of the Olympics—the four-horse chariot race.

Abby and Doc stood at the top of the slope, at the very back of the crowd. They could sort of see the field from there, if they stood on tiptoes. Plus, they could stay out of sight of the judges.

"They're right up front," Doc said, pointing to the men in purple robes standing alongside the race track.

"We shall be fine here, children," said the bearded man standing beside Abby and Doc.

At least, they hoped it looked like a
bearded man.

Actually, it was Kyniska, wearing the fake
beard Sally had bought the day before. She
hadn't planned to sneak in—the judges really
did threaten to throw women who broke the
rules off the side of a mountain. But when
Doc and Abby told her their plan, she liked it.
She *had* to see it for herself.

The entire arena buzzed with energy—men bragging about their knowledge of the drivers and teams, arguing over who would win, challenging friends to bets.

Trumpets blared. Everyone turned toward the hippodrome's arched entryway.

"Now begins the procession," Kyniska explained. "Each team will ride in and be introduced by the herald."

In single file, the chariots rolled into the arena. Each was pulled by four horses, their muscles bulging, coats gleaming in the sunlight. In each chariot stood a proud man in long white robes, reins in one hand, a whip in the other. A man with an amazingly loud voice announced the name of each team owner and driver, and where they were born.

"Here she comes!" Abby cried.

The crowd gasped.

The final chariot rolled slowly into the

hippodrome. Like the others, it was pulled by four horses.

But it was a bit larger than your regulation Olympic chariot.

It was a red Lockheed Vega.

Amelia Earhart waved to the crowd. She'd opened the top of the cockpit, which allowed her to stand with her head and chest above the top of the plane. She was wearing her leather flight helmet, with hair tucked in and goggles over her eyes.

"And here is the team of Kyniska of Sparta!" the herald's voice echoed through the stands. "Driven by . . ."

He checked his notes.

"Driven by Earhart of Kansas. Wherever that is."

The crowd cheered.

Woo-hoo! Yeah! Bring it on!

"And now," continued the herald. "All teams will take their places at the starting line to await the starting trumpet!"

The teams—thirty of them—crowded together at one end of the track.

"The race is twelve laps around the

hippodrome," Kyniska told Doc and Abby. "First racer to cross the finish line wins. A lifetime of hopes and dreams and work—and it will all be over in fifteen minutes."

"She'll win," Doc said.

Kyniska took a deep breath. "We shall see . . ."

The trumpeter raised his horn and blasted.

CHAPTER FOURTEEN

The horses bolted forward.

Fans stood and roared as the teams dashed down the track, kicking up clouds of dust.

"Notice how the crowds are biggest at each end of the stadium?" Kyniska shouted to Abby and Doc. "Everyone wants to see the turns—where most of the crashes happen."

The horses barely slowed as they rounded the first turn. Sure enough, one of the carts skidded sideways and slammed into the low wooden wall around the track. The driver sailed into the crowd.

Abby and Doc jumped up and down—both with excitement and to get a better view.

"Go, Amelia!" Abby yelped. "I mean, Earhart!"

But Earhart was falling behind. As she rounded the stone pillar and started back up the track, several teams pulled past her.

At the front of the pack, drivers screamed at their teams. Competing horses slammed their sides against each other, fighting for position. One chariot side-swiped the chariot next to it, the wheels grinding together.

Both drivers lifted their whips and starting whipping each other.

"Hey, can you do that?" Abby asked.

"It happens," Kyniska said.

"What a crazy sport!" Doc shouted.

Galloping hooves thundered on the track, and the drivers were screaming, and everyone was covered in sweat and dust. As

they rounded the next turn, two of the lead
chariots slammed together, and the wheels
of one of the chariots shattered. The cart
tipped forward and bounced off the dirt,
and the driver somersaulted into the path of
onrushing teams. He leaped up and dodged
the horses, but not one of the chariots. The
man howled as a speeding wheel bounced
over his foot.

"That's gonna leave a mark," Doc said.

"Come on, Earhart!" Abby shouted. "Faster!"

Amelia's Vega rounded the turn in dead last.

Abby pointed. "She falling too far behind!"

"It's the flying chariot," Kyniska said. "It's too heavy for the horses."

"We were afraid of that," Doc said.

The horses were working hard but falling farther and farther behind. After six laps, Amelia was so far in back of the leaders they were coming up behind her. She watched as one chariot after another sped past her plane.

The plan was failing.

Amelia turned to the crowd, looking around.

"She's looking for us," Abby said.

"Up here!" Doc called, jumping and waving.

Amelia shouted something, pointing to the team of horses.

"What'd she say?" Doc asked.

"Can't hear," Abby said. "Let's get closer."

They shoved their way through the crowd. By the time they got to the front, Amelia was two full laps behind the pack.

"Three laps to go!" shouted the herald.

Abby and Doc watched the horses and chariots speed past. Amelia's team rode by at a slow trot.

"Here!" Doc yelled to Amelia. "We're over here!"

"New plan!" Amelia shouted. "Cut me loose!"

"Do *not* go out there," warned Kyniska, who'd pushed her way to the front. "Far too dangerous."

"Untie the horses!" Amelia yelled. "It's my only chance!"

The fans were on their feet, whooping and screeching.

Abby and Doc nodded to each other, then darted onto the track.

The herald bellowed, "Two laps to go!"

Amelia pulled on her reins, and the team came to a stop. She threw the reins down to Doc.

"Easy, guys," Doc told the horses, patting their noses. He liked horses. He'd been a cowboy once. For a few minutes.

Abby dove between the wheels of the plane and started to untie the rope holding the plane to the team of horses.

"Hurry!" Doc shouted.

Abby looked down the track. The leading teams were rounding the stone pillar and rumbling her way.

She yanked out the last loop in the knot. The rope fell to the ground. Kyniska whistled and the horses ran to her.

Doc gave Amelia a thumbs-up.

Amelia dropped into the seat of her plane. The engine coughed. Black smoke shot out.

The propeller spun slowly, slowly—then burst into a whirl.

The plane bounced down the field, picking up speed, and lifted into the air.

CHAPTER FIFTEEN

Abby and Doc dashed to the side of the track and leaped back into the stands. Panting like dogs, they watched Amelia's plane climb above the hills near the hippodrome.

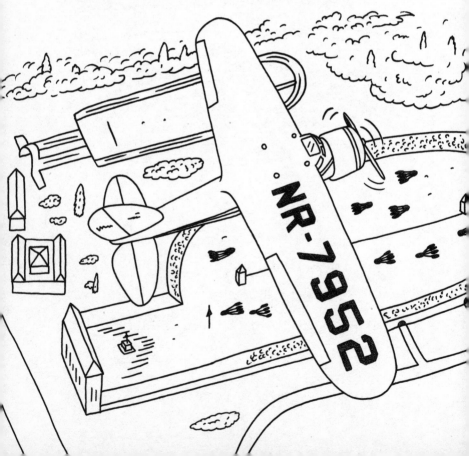

"There she goes," Abby said.

"Why didn't she take us?" Doc asked.

"Don't know," Abby said, noticing the judges standing nearby. Several of them were glaring at her and Doc.

Amelia's plane turned back toward the hippodrome.

"She's coming back!" Doc called.

"She's not escaping?" Abby wondered. "Seems like a good time to escape."

The plane buzzed over the track, just a hundred feet off the ground. Amelia tore past all the chariots, reached the far end of the field in seconds, and banked into a sharp turn over the stone pillar.

Kyniska's face burst into a smile. "She's going to try to win the race!"

Amelia came roaring down the track. Fans looked up, pointing and cheering.

"Final lap!" cried the herald. "Final lap!"

As drivers called furiously to their horses,

Amelia flew tight laps over the track, passing the chariots again and again. The teams in front rounded the far pole and swung back up the track toward the finish line.

Amelia's plane was right behind them.

Forty thousand fans stomped and shrieked.

Kyniska was shouting the loudest.

Amelia tilted her plane's nose down, diving

to gain speed. She zipped just feet above the lead teams, roaring past the finish line for the win.

"Yes!" Doc shouted.

Abby jumped up and down, shouting, "Earhart! Earhart!"

Kyniska grabbed them both in a rough embrace.

"I won!" she whooped. "I am the champion!"

———•———

The dust was still settling in the hippodrome as Amelia Earhart set her plane down.

The track looked like a battlefield.

Pieces of chariots littered the dirt. Drivers hobbled off the field. A few lay on the ground while doctors wrapped bandages around arms and legs and heads.

"The judges will now present the prize to the winner," Kyniska told Doc and Abby.

"Just what we need," Doc said. "Another olive wreath."

The wreath from yesterday was still in his back pocket, hidden by his T-shirt.

"Normally, the owner would be on the field with the driver," Kyniska said. Touching her beard, she added, "However, since I am not actually permitted to be here . . ."

"I'm still mad about that," Abby said.

Kyniska laughed. "The true glory is being the champion. There will be parades when I return home. There will be statues of me, poems in my honor. Look—here come the judges with the prize!"

Four men in purple robes carried a golden table toward Amelia's airplane. There was something on the table. It was not an olive wreath.

It was a hat. A tall black hat.

"That sort of looks like . . ." Doc said.

"But it couldn't be . . ." Abby said.

"What?" Kyniska demanded. "What is that thing?"

"I don't know," Abby said. "It looks like Abraham Lincoln's hat."

CHAPTER SIXTEEN

The judges set the table down. One of the judges raised his arms, and the fans quieted down.

"It is now time to present the prize to the winner!" another judge announced. "But the sacred wreath for this glorious event has been stolen!"

The crowd hissed and booed.

"Indeed, it is a terrible thing!" the judge continued. "However, when we went to get the prize this morning, we found that someone—perhaps Zeus himself—had replaced the missing wreath with this very special object!"

The judge lifted the black hat. The crowd gasped.

"We believe," he told the stunned crowd,

"it is meant to be worn on the head!"

And he put the hat on. "How do I look?"

"Absurd," said a fellow judge.

He took the hat off.

"I now present this extraordinary prize," proclaimed the judge, "to Kyniska, Princess of Sparta, and to her driver, Earhart of Kansas!"

Amelia stood in her plane, waving to the crowd.

She pulled off her goggles and helmet. Her hair flapped in the breeze.

"Ah, much better," she said. "First, let me congratulate the other teams for a marvelous race!"

The entire arena went silent. The judges looked at each other.

"Is Earhart a woman?" one asked.

"She looks like a woman."

"She *sounds* like a woman."

Forty thousand fans stood, staring at Amelia.

"Oops," Amelia said, remembering the no-women rule.

"Time to get out of here," Abby suggested.

Doc nodded. "Let's grab the hat, too. In case it's really Abe's."

"Good idea," Abby agreed. "Well, congrats again," she said to Kyniska.

"Thank you, children," Kyniska said. "Hurry!"

Abby and Doc hopped onto the track and sprinted toward the prize table.

"The wreath thieves!" shouted one of the judges. "Stop them!"

Doc pulled the wreath from his pocket and tossed it. "We didn't steal it!"

The wreath hit the judge in the nose.

Abby snatched the hat off the table.

"Put that back!" cried the judge.

"In!" Amelia shouted, holding open the door of her plane. "Get in!"

Doc dove in, followed by Abby. The judges lunged toward the door—which slammed shut in their faces. The plane jolted forward.

Judges in flowing purple robes ran after the

plane, waving and yelling. Fans poured from the stands to join the chase. Drivers jumped back into their chariots and sped alongside the plane, smacking the wings with their whips.

Amelia's plane rattled and bounced as it gained speed. But it was running out of runway, fast approaching the end of the track—and the stone pillar. With only a few feet to spare, the plane lifted into the air.

Thousands of furious faces watched the flying chariot climb, turn, and sail over the hills of Olympia.

The only one smiling was Kyniska.

"Nice flying!" Abby shouted.

"Thank you, Abby," said Amelia Earhart. "It wasn't bad, if I say so myself."

Abby and Doc sat on the bench behind the cockpit. When their hearts stopped racing, they started to think about the tall black hat Abby held in her lap.

"It really *does* look like Abraham Lincoln's," she said.

"Look inside," Doc said. "Remember how he keeps notes and stuff in his hat?"

Abby turned the hat upside down. Folded pieces of paper were stuck in the lining.

Doc took one out and read the note aloud:

"The next time someone tells me my jacket is too short, I should say, 'Well, it will be a lot *longer* before I get a new one.'"

Doc looked up from the paper. "Is that supposed to be a joke?"

"I think so," Abby said. "A lot *longer*. Get it? A *longer* time before he gets a new coat?"

"I'm not putting that back," Doc said.

He crumpled the paper and tossed it under the bench.

"It's Lincoln's hat all right!" Abby said, loud enough for Amelia to hear.

Amelia turned and said, "How is that possible?"

"Who knows?" Abby asked.

"We should return it," Doc said.

"Maybe we'll suddenly appear there, in Lincoln's time," Abby said. "I mean, we had the wreath, and we just appeared in ancient Greece, right?"

"Yeah," Doc said. "That actually makes sense."

Amelia Earhart shook her head. "*None* of this makes sense."

"Okay, we're ready!" Doc shouted. "Take us to Mr. Lincoln!"

Abby yelled into the hat. "Hello in there! Can you hear us?"

Nothing happened.

The plane flew over the rocky hills of Greece and soared toward the Mediterranean coast.

CHAPTER SEVENTEEN

"It's not working," Doc said.

"Anytime now!" Abby told the hat. "We're ready to go!"

Amelia asked, "Who on earth are you talking to?"

"We have no idea," Doc said.

"Wonderful," Amelia muttered.

Abby said, "Other history people, you know, Lincoln, Abigail Adams. They figured out ways to move around in time."

"You mean, I could go home anytime I want?" Amelia asked.

"Maybe," Abby said.

Doc laughed. "Remember the desert island, with the pirates chasing us? And Abigail and John Adams jumped into that barrel?"

Abby smiled. "They almost had us."

"Barrel?" Amelia said.

"Yeah," Doc said, "like a wooden thing, for holding water or—"

"I know what a barrel is," Amelia cut in. "It's just . . . you've given me an idea . . ."

She stared straight ahead, lost in thought.

Then, turning to Doc and Abby, she said, "Let's go find Mr. Lincoln."

"We should go back to your time," Abby said. "If you can, I mean. So you can do your flight."

"Not yet," Amelia said. "First we're going to figure out exactly what's going on. And, Abby, I haven't forgotten about finding your glasses."

"Thanks," Abby said.

"What about my hat?" Doc asked. "How come no one cares about my hat?"

"Here we go, to wherever Mr. Lincoln is," Amelia said. "Hold on tight, children. This is called a barrel roll."

"A wha—?" Doc started to ask.

WHAAAAAAA!

The plane flipped over and flew upside down.

Abby and Doc screamed as the plane rolled over and over—right side up, then upside down, right side up, then upside down—and disappeared.

———•———

And reappeared in a cloudy sky. Doc and Abby were still gripping the bench.

Abby hooted, "Best ride ever!"

"It worked!" Doc shouted. "Or, did it? Is this Washington, DC?"

Amelia looked to both sides and straight ahead. Nothing in sight but clouds.

"I can't tell," she said. "But it's not a good day for flying."

The plane bounced in the wind as it dropped through the clouds. A city came into view. Brick buildings and church steeples. Dirt streets laid out in neat square blocks. Wooden ships docked on a wide river. The lower they got, the less it looked like Washington. There was no Capitol building, no White House.

Amelia picked out an open field just outside the city and brought the plane in for a bumpy landing. Doc and Abby hopped out and looked up at the dark rain clouds.

"Storm's coming," Abby said.

"At least we have a hat," Doc said, setting the tall black hat on his head.

A voice boomed,

I believe that belongs to me!

Abby and Doc spun around.

A tall man in a black suit was walking toward them. He had a beard but no mustache. It was Abraham Lincoln.

Didn't think you could have all this fun without me, did you?

Abby clapped. "We found you!"

"You did, indeed," Lincoln said, smiling and shaking their hands.

"But we're not in Washington," Doc said.

"Philadelphia," Lincoln said. "Fall of 1753."

"What are you doing here?" Abby asked.

Lincoln reached into his jacket and pulled out something brown and furry. He put it on his head.

It was a thick fur hat.
A long tail hung from the
back.

"Who do I look like?"
Lincoln asked.

Abby and Doc were
stumped.

"Famous writer, scientist, diplomat, one
of our country's founders . . ." Lincoln said.
"Picture me with long hair and a bit, um," he
patted his belly, "rounder."

Amelia Earhart stuck her head out of the
plane. "Benjamin Franklin!"

"We have a winner!" Lincoln called, tossing
her the fur hat. "Nice to meet you, Ms.
Earhart."

"Likewise," she said. "Do you really believe
this is Franklin's?"

Lincoln took his own hat from Doc and set
it on his head.

He said, "Let's go find out."

CHAPTER EIGHTEEN

The sky was growing darker. Thunder rumbled.

Abby, Doc, Amelia Earhart, and Abraham Lincoln walked through the streets of Philadelphia. Abby asked for directions to Franklin's home. It was a three-story brick house, with a tall metal pole sticking up from the roof. Doc knocked on the front door.

The door opened. Benjamin Franklin stood in the doorway. He wore a vest and a puffy white shirt, and he had brown hair down to his shoulders.

For just an instant, his face showed a hint of alarm.

But then he smiled and said, "Come inside, friends, please."

They all stepped inside. Abe Lincoln and
Amelia Earhart introduced themselves.

"Yes, of course," Ben said, shaking their
hands. "We've been in many history books
together. How nice to finally meet. And you
two—you must be Doc and Abby. The ones
who broke history!"

"It was his fault, too," Doc said, pointing to
Lincoln.

Franklin laughed. "I admire curious children. I myself have a—what are you staring at, child?"

"It's just . . ." Abby began. "You're not old. In pictures, you're always old."

"Yes, and bald into the bargain!" Ben howled. "When children think of Benjamin Franklin, what do they think of? Electricity and lightning? The kite experiment? Well, I'll have you know I conducted that experiment last year, when I was a man of but six and forty! With nice, wavy hair! Why can't your books show that?"

"Um . . ." Doc said.

"Well, no matter," Ben said, smiling again. "To what do I owe the pleasure of this visit?"

Abe Lincoln held out the fur hat. "Might this belong to you, Franklin?"

Franklin took the hat. Again, worry flashed across his face.

Everyone noticed.

"Yes, thank you," Ben said. "Things have been getting rather twisted up lately, haven't they?"

"Indeed," Abe said. "This morning, when I reached for my hat, it was gone! And your hat was on the shelf in its place. Can you explain what it was doing in the White House? In 1861?"

Ben shook his head. "I truly cannot."

"But you seem to know *something*," Doc said.

"Do I?" Ben laughed nervously. "Well . . . perhaps a little something."

"Out with it, Franklin," Abe insisted.

"Please," Amelia urged. "I'm in a hurry to cross the Atlantic."

"It's quite amusing, actually," Ben began. "You see, after my famous kite experiment— you know about that, right? I wanted to show that electricity forms in storm clouds and that this is what causes lightning. So as a storm approached, my son William and I flew a kite."

"The kite was not hit by lightning," Ben continued. "That would have killed us. But an electrical charge did travel down the string to a metal key, thus proving my theory, and—"

"Get to the point," Amelia pleaded.

"Of course," Ben said. "I saw what Lincoln and Abigail Adams did, traveling through time, becoming wrestlers, pirates, such adventures! That gave me an idea for a new experiment. Could one use electricity to, well, *zap* history?"

"*Zap*?" Abby asked. "Is that the scientific word?"

"Perhaps not," Ben said. "But you see, I recently put a lightning rod on my roof— my own invention, by the way. The pole attracts lightning, and wires carry the charge harmlessly into the ground. The electricity can also be used for experiments. I attached wires to two books—one about cowboys and one about astronauts. I waited for the next storm and, well, the lightning did the rest!"

"So that's how Neil Armstrong and Buzz Aldrin wound up landing in Texas instead of on the moon?" Doc asked.

Ben beamed with pride. "I had no idea the results would be so dramatic!"

"Wait," Abby said. "How'd you get books about things that haven't happened yet?"

Ben opened his mouth to answer, but Amelia cut in: "And *that's* how I wound up at the ancient Olympics!"

"No, Ms. Earhart, a thousand times, no," Ben said. "I had nothing to do with that. I saw how much trouble I had caused for the astronauts and decided never to repeat the experiment."

Everyone stared at Ben Franklin.

"You must believe me," he insisted.

They didn't.

"Come see for yourself," Ben said. "My study is right above us."

Ben Franklin led the way up a creaking staircase. Rain began pounding on the roof.

He opened the door of his study. The large room was lit by the flickering flames of lanterns. The shelves were packed with books. A long table was lined with glass tubes and jars of colorful liquids. Jumbles of wires dangled from a hole in the ceiling and snaked from one piece of lab equipment to another. Thunder cracked in the sky.

A girl stood at the table.

She was wearing Abby's glasses.

And Doc's hat.

"Hi, Abby," Sally said. "Hi, Doc."

CHAPTER NINETEEN

"We, uh . . ." Abby stammered. "We thought you went home."

"I *am* home!" Sally said.

"Hold on . . ." Abby said.

Doc asked, "What do you mean, you're home?"

Ben Franklin stepped into the lab. "I see you've met my favorite lab partner. My daughter, Sarah. We call her Sally."

"You're Sally *Franklin*?" Doc asked.

"Ben Franklin is your *dad*?" Abby asked.

Sally smiled. "Did I not mention that?"

Abby and Doc shook their heads.

"Well, it's true." She took off the hat and glasses and held them out. "Here."

Abby took off her goofy glasses and put on her good ones.

"So," Doc said, adjusting his hat. "You did all this?"

"I told you I go to your school library sometimes," Sally said. "I saw those pictures on the wall from Halloween and saw your costumes, Amelia Earhart and the Olympic champion. So I came up with this time twister, just for you!"

"Um . . . thanks?" Abby said.

"Mixing up people's glasses and goggles and hats and wreaths," Sally explained, "that's easy if you know how to get around. I took the books back here and hooked them up to my father's invention."

Sally pointed to two books on the table—an Amelia Earhart biography and a book about the ancient Olympic games. Both had stickers that show where they go on the library shelf.

"Lightning struck and *POOF*!" Sally cried. "You're off to ancient Greece! Then I couldn't resist going, too. But I didn't mean to break Kyniska's chariot. Is she still mad?"

"No," Abby said. "Thanks to Amelia Earhart."

"Oh, good," Sally said. "Switching my father's hat with Lincoln's—that was a little bonus. And you figured it out! Wasn't it fun?"

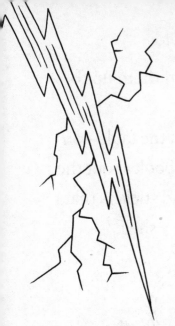

Abby and Doc looked at each other and smiled. It *was* fun, actually. Tiring, but fun.

A slash of lightning filled the room with light. Thunder boomed a second later.

"Storm's getting closer," Amelia said.

"Allow me to apologize," Ben said to Abby and Doc. "And to you, Ms. Earhart. I had no idea Sally was doing these experiments. But one must admit, they show a certain greatness of mind!"

"I suppose," Amelia said. "In any case, it's quite all right. Though I really should be getting back to my—"

"Excuse me," Abe jumped in, "but it's *not* all right. Franklin, you must promise to never do this again. You, too, Sally."

"So you get to sail with pirates and ride with cowboys," Sally snapped. "And I'm just supposed to sit around here learning how to sew?"

Ben chuckled. "She's got you there, Lincoln."

"I know, I know, I started this," Abe said. "I am to blame. But it has to end, here and now!"

And he pulled the wires out of a tube filled with something green.

"Stop that!" Franklin ordered. "You're not the president here!"

"Help me take this apart." Lincoln grabbed a green jar.

"Put it down!" Franklin roared.

The jar fell and shattered. Green liquid soaked Abe's and Ben's shoes.

Franklin clenched his fists. "You come into my home! Order me around! Smash my custom glassware!"

"I'm sorry," Abe said, yanking the wires from another jar. "It must be done."

Ben charged, seizing Abe around the waist.

Leave my stuff alone!

"I'm not the man to trifle with," Abe warned, the wires still in his fist. "I'll have you know, I'm in the Wrestling Hall of Fame."

"Good for you," Ben grunted. "I'm in the Swimming Hall of Fame!"

"You're making that up!"

"Look it up, Lincoln!"

Abe wrapped his long arms around Ben's thick chest just as—*CRACK!!!*—lightning struck the rod on the roof.

The room lit up and thunder echoed and the wires in Abe's hands sizzled and sparked.

Both men tumbled to the floor.

The room filled with smoke and the awful smell of burning hair.

CHAPTER TWENTY

Lincoln and Franklin lay on the floor in a tangle of limbs. Both were groaning.

Slowly, the smoke cleared.

Abe pulled his arm out from under Ben. He sat up. "Are you quite all right, Franklin?"

"I believe so, thank you."

Abe helped Ben sit up and brushed the dust from his back. They were both okay.

Except for one minor detail.

Ben Franklin now had a beard—Lincoln's famous chin beard. And on his head was Lincoln's wild black hair.

Why does my face suddenly feel itchy?

Abe Lincoln had Franklin's hair—bald in front, with long, wavy strands around the sides and back. No beard.

Neither had noticed. Yet.

Sally covered her mouth. Abby and Doc bit their lips to keep from cracking up.

"Stop staring, children," Ben grumbled. "I've given myself worse jolts than that many times."

"We were lucky," Lincoln said. "But let this be a lesson to us—no more toying with history!"

Franklin waved away the idea. "Nonsense, Lincoln. We'll have many more adventures. And from now on, I shall be one of the main characters!"

"You? Why?"

"You want children to like history—isn't that how this all began? Well, who in history is more fun than me?" Turning to Doc and Abby, he said, "Did you know, I once wrote a scientific paper on farting!"

"Is that something to be proud of?" Abe asked.

"You know nothing of humor, Lincoln. I've heard your jokes."

"Sorry to interrupt this important discussion, gentlemen," Amelia Earhart cut in. "I've got an ocean to cross."

"Yes, yes, bon voyage!" Ben said.

"Safe travels, Ms. Earhart," Abe added.

Amelia, Sally, Abby, and Doc raced down the stairs, burst out the door—and exploded in laughter, giggling so hard they fell to the sidewalk.

———•———

The storm was moving off to the south. The sky was getting brighter.

Sally waved to Amelia Earhart's red Vega as it rose above Philadelphia. She watched the plane go into a barrel roll—and disappear.

BLINK.

Bon voyage! Have a safe trip!

Moments later, Amelia brought the plane in for a soft landing on the soccer field outside Abby and Doc's school.

The door opened. Abby and Doc stumbled out.

Amelia slid her cockpit window open. "Remember," she said, shouting over her spinning propeller.

When a great adventure is offered, don't refuse it!

"We won't!" Doc yelled.

"Thanks, Amelia!" Abby shouted. "For everything!"

Amelia Earhart waved and slid the window

shut. Her plane sped down the soccer field, took off, climbed, and went into another barrel roll—

And was gone.

Abby and Doc stood for a minute, gazing up at the blue sky.

Then they went inside to find their mom. She was in her classroom, sitting at her desk.

"Ah, finally," she said, shoving aside a stack of papers. "Good to see you found the glasses, Abby."

"And my hat," Doc said.

"Right, Doc, the hat," their mom said, smiling. "Can we please go home now?"

CHAPTER
TWENTY-ONE

Abby and Doc slept through most of the weekend.

On Monday morning, before class, they took their history books from their desks and flipped to the page about Amelia Earhart.

"She made it across the Atlantic," Abby said. "Landed safely in Ireland."

Doc read aloud:

And with that historic flight, Amelia Earhart became one of the most famous and admired women in the world.

"Sounds right," Abby said with a sigh of relief.

"We did it again," Doc said. "Fixed history!"

"Did we?" Abby asked. "Check Lincoln."

Doc flipped to the section about Abraham Lincoln.

The president was locked in his bedroom in the White House. He was refusing to come out.

"Guess he's still got Franklin's hair," Doc said. "Poor guy."

"It's not the best look," Abby agreed.

R-I-I-I-I-N-G!

Ms. Maybee stood in front of the class. "All right, guys, I hope you had a wonderful weekend. Now, before we get started, I want you all to give a warm welcome to a new student who'll be joining our class!"

Ms. Maybee pointed to the back of the room.

Everyone turned to see the new girl.

"Hi, I'm Sarah," she said.

But everyone calls me Sally!

UN-TWISTING HISTORY

Amelia Earhart did a lot of amazing things. Competing at the ancient Olympics was not one of them.

But there's a lot of stuff in this book that really *is* true.

As I'm sure you know, Amelia Earhart really was a famous pilot. She really did fly across the Atlantic Ocean in 1928, becoming the first woman to do it. As she tells Abby and Doc in Chapter Twelve, she was basically a passenger—"a sack of potatoes," as she said at the time. Always pushing herself to take on new challenges, she flew the ocean again in 1932—this time solo—becoming the first woman to cross the Atlantic alone.

Amelia's conversation with reporters in Chapter Three is directly based on the kinds of things she said all the time. Some of her lines are word-for-word quotes, including the classic: "Women, like men, should try to do the impossible. And when they fail, their failure should be a challenge to others."

That quote sums up Amelia Earhart's approach to life. It explains why she's such a huge hero to kids, including Abby—and my own daughter, Anna. And to adults, too, like me.

It wasn't the safest way to live, though.

In 1937, while attempting to become the first pilot to fly around the world along the equator, Amelia Earhart disappeared. What happened? That's one of history's all-time great mysteries. Most likely, Earhart and her navigator, Fred Noonan, were unable to find the tiny Pacific island they were planning to land on. The plane probably ran out of fuel and went down at sea.

But people are *still* looking for Amelia

Earhart, *still* coming up with theories to explain her disappearance. More importantly, I think, people are still celebrating her life and achievements. As soon as I thought of the idea for Time Twisters, I knew she'd play a starring role.

Now, on to the ancient Olympics.

Doc's gross details about Olympia—the smells, the lack of bathrooms, boxers swallowing their own teeth—that's all based on historical accounts of the ancient games. And yes, athletes did compete naked. The explanation Doc gives in Chapter Six is based on a legend that may or may not be true. But we know it's true that the chariot racers were the exception—they wore robes because racers got thrown from their chariots all the time, and the robes offered some small protection. The details about women being excluded from the Olympics are also true. They could not compete, or even enter the arena to watch.

Which brings us to Kyniska, a real-life Spartan princess who refused to be told there was something she couldn't do. As the owner and trainer of a chariot team, Kyniska won the Olympic chariot race in the year 396 BCE. Then she won it again four years later. Just as she told Doc and Abby, there were poems in her honor, and parades, and a statue at Olympia with the inscription: "My ancestors and brothers were kings of Sparta. I, Kyniska, victorious with a chariot of swift-footed horses, erected this statue. I declare that I am the only woman in all of Greece to have won this crown."

What about Sarah Franklin? Sally, as her family called her.

We don't know very much about Sally's childhood, but we know that she loved to read the books in her famous father's library. We know Benjamin Franklin bragged in letters about Sally being very smart and very funny. And we know she was nine years old at the time of her father's famous kite experiment. Nine—the same age as Abby and Doc! I decided she'd be the perfect person to be the brains behind this time-twisting adventure.

Finally, a few words about Ben Franklin's electrical experiments. In Chapter Twenty, he was telling the truth when he said, "I've given myself worse jolts than that many times." Franklin loved to experiment with electricity and early versions of batteries, and he had a few dangerous accidents. In the famous kite experiment, conducted in June 1752, he and his twenty-one-year-old son, William, flew a kite as a thunderstorm was rolling into town. Franklin wanted to show that lightning *was* electricity, and that it could travel from object to object. As the kite neared the storm cloud, an electrical charge traveled down the wet kite string to a metal key—and jumped from the key to Ben's hand.

He was lucky not to be hurt. If lightning had struck the kite—as often shown in inaccurate drawings of this event—whoever was holding the string would have been killed. Several people died doing the same experiment.

Seriously, don't try this at home.

And yes, it's absolutely true that Franklin once wrote a scientific essay called "Fart Proudly." It was his way of goofing on scientists who took themselves too seriously.

Oh, and one more thing. Benjamin Franklin really is in the International Swimming Hall of Fame.

Look it up.

CREDITS

STEVE SHEINKIN, *Author*

NEIL SWAAB, *Interior Illustrator / Designer*

OLIVIA ASERR, *Cover Illustrator*

MIKE BURROUGHS, *Cover Letterer*

CONNIE HSU, *Executive Editor*

JEN BESSER, *Publisher*

ELIZABETH CLARK, *Creative Director*

TOM NAU, *Director of Production*

JILL FRESHNEY, *Senior Executive Managing Editor*

MEGAN ABBATE, *Assistant Editor*

What did you want to be when you grew up? My younger brother and I spent most of our childhood writing stories and making "shows"—comedy sketches that we'd videotape. I've seen some of the tapes recently. They're not that funny. But we thought they were, and I became convinced I was going to be some kind of writer.

What's your most embarrassing childhood memory? I cried pretty much the entire first day of first grade. It was a new school, and I really didn't want to be there. A lot of kids, even my friends, never let me forget that day . . .

What's your favorite childhood memory? I once got a metal detector as a present, and it was so exciting to use it in my yard. I was absolutely sure I'd find buried treasure! I didn't. But still, to this day I can't resist any story about buried treasure.

What was your favorite thing about school? When a teacher would tell us stories. I didn't care if it was a fictional epic like *The Odyssey*, or something from history, or just a true story from the teacher's own life. Almost any story at all held my attention.

Did you play sports as a kid? I always loved playing sports with friends, but was never super serious about being on teams. In middle school and high school I was on the cross-country team, because that was one sport that welcomed the very skinny.

What was your first job, and what was your "worst" job? I've had so many terrible jobs, far too many to list, and that's one reason I'm so happy now being a writer. I started with the usual lawn mowing. To me, the worst jobs were in restaurants, where you had to act happy in front of the customers. My bosses kept telling me, "You don't smile enough!"

How did you celebrate publishing your first book? The day I found out my first book was going to be published was the *exact* same day I found out my wife and I were going to have a daughter. So the daughter news sort of won out, and rightfully so.

Where do you write your books? I used to go to my public library. I'd sit in the exact same seat and stay there all day. After I had a few books published, I was able to afford to rent a tiny office. I like getting out of the house, because I feel like I'm really going to work.

What sparked your imagination for the Time Twisters series? Well, I don't like to admit it, because I'm afraid kids will get mad, but I used to write history textbooks for a living. I always felt sorry for the historical figures who were stuck in those boring books, doing the same thing over and over. That led to the idea of letting them escape and go on adventures in other times and places.

What challenges do you face in the writing process, and how do you overcome them? As much as I love my job, I do think the writing process is pretty hard. It takes a lot of discipline to put in the hours needed to write something good.

What's the best advice you have ever received about writing? "Keep going." It sounds so simple, but it's the hardest part. Just keep working, no matter what.

What would you do if you ever stopped writing? At this point, I'm not really qualified to do anything else.

If you could live in any fictional world, what would it be? I'd want to be on a pirate ship of some kind, like in one of my favorite books, *Treasure Island*. I know real-life pirates were cruel and disgusting, but in fictional adventures it seems like a lot of fun.

If you could travel in time, where would you go and what would you do? This fantasy is such a key part of the Time Twisters. I get to send my characters to meet people like Abe Lincoln and Amelia Earhart, to ride with cowboys and see the ancient Olympics. A big part of making up the stories is asking myself, "Where would you like to go next?"

If you were a superhero, what would your superpower be? Funny you should ask, because my daughter and I have been talking about this over breakfast and we came up with a great one. And by "great" I mean hilariously lame. It's Non-Fiction Man! He has the power to convince kids history is exciting! At least, he thinks he does. He and his daughter set out on adventures, and of course things go terribly wrong . . .

OH NO! FAMOUS FOLKS FROM HISTORY
KNOW THEY DON'T HAVE TO DO THE SAME
OLD THING ANYMORE—AND EVERYTHING IS
TWISTING OUT OF CONTROL!

FIND OUT WHAT HAPPENS IN THE OTHER
TIME TWISTERS ADVENTURES:

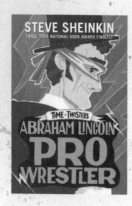  

KEEP READING FOR AN EXCERPT FROM
ABRAHAM LINCOLN, PRO WRESTLER . . .

CHAPTER ONE

Ms. Maybee said, "Okay, guys, let's get out our history books!"

The whole class groaned.

Doc tilted his head back and started snoring.

"Very funny," Ms. Maybee said. "This is going to be fun, trust me. Abby? How about if you get us started."

Abby—she's the one who broke history. It was Abby and her stepbrother, Doc.

You can thank them later.

ABBY   DOC

ZZZZZZZ

Everyone took out their textbooks. Thick books. Heavy. Kids lifted them high and let them drop onto their desks. It sounded like thunder.

Ms. Maybee just shook her head.

"Page one twenty-five," she said. "Today we'll read about Abraham Lincoln."

More groans. And Doc sang out, "Bor—ing!"

Ms. Maybee glared at the class. "Who said that?"

Everyone knew. But no one said.

"Well, whoever it was," Ms. Maybee said, looking right at Doc, "you should be aware that you are not only rude, but also totally wrong."

She pointed to a poster of Abraham Lincoln taped to the classroom wall.

"Abraham Lincoln is one of our most important presidents," she said. "He basically saved the country and ended slavery. And he's certainly *not* boring. Come on, you'll see." And she said, "Abby, when you're ready."

Abby opened the textbook to page 125. There was an old black-and-white picture of a house with a horse and wagon driving by. She read what it said at the top of the page: "Lincoln: from Lawyer to President."

"A little louder, Abby," Ms. Maybee said. "We're going to show these people how exciting history can be!"

She read louder: "Abraham Lincoln sat at a large desk in his office in the city of Springfield, Illinois. He was reading a newspaper. After a little while, he put the newspaper down and stood up. He walked out of the room. He came back carrying a cup of coffee. He sat down again. He picked up the newspaper and began to read."

Abby looked up from the book, pretty confused.

"See," Doc said. "Nap time."

For once, Ms. Maybee didn't yell at him. "Okay," she said, "that wasn't the most thrilling part, I'll admit. Doc, since you're so interested, why don't you see what comes next?"

He read aloud: "Abraham Lincoln turned to the next page of the newspaper. He took a sip of coffee. He put his feet up on his desk. He read some more. Every few minutes he sipped his drink."

Doc stopped. "Do I have to keep going?" he asked.

"No, that's fine," Ms. Maybee said.

She looked at her own copy of the textbook. "According to what it says here, he just sat at his desk all day. He read the paper, drank coffee, and, um, that's it. That's all he did."

"Why do we have to know this stuff?" Doc asked.

"It's important," Ms. Maybee said.

"Why?"

"It just is," she said. "Hmmm . . ." She was still looking at her book. "This really doesn't seem right. I remember Lincoln *doing* a lot more. But to be totally honest, history was never my favorite subject."

"Because it's boring!" Doc said.

"Well, this book is a little dry, I'll admit," Ms. Maybee said.

She closed the textbook and said, "Let's do a math worksheet."

And a few kids actually cheered.

CHAPTER TWO

When the school day ended, Abby walked through the library to the storage room in the back. It was a small room packed with books—books on shelves, in cardboard boxes, and stacked up on the floor. There were two chairs and a table and one small window.

Abby sat and started taking stuff out of her backpack.

This happened every day. Abby and Doc's mother was a teacher at the school and ran an after-school program for younger kids. Their dad taught at the middle school and stayed late to coach track. So every day, after school, Abby and Doc had to stick around for about an hour, until their mom was ready to leave. They were supposed to sit in this room and do homework or read.

It was usually the longest hour of the day. Not this time.

Doc came in and tossed down his backpack. He stepped onto a chair, then onto the table, and from there he climbed onto one of the stacks of boxes. His head almost touched the ceiling.

Think I could jump from here to that big box?

He pointed to a tall box about six feet away.

"Probably," Abby said. "But I'm not saying you'd live."

"I'm the Amazing, um, no, I'm Doctor Frog-Leg!"

"You are?"

"Well, that's my pro-wrestling name," he said.

That was the big thing in school that week. There was going to be a pro-wrestling tournament in the gym Friday night, and kids were joking about what their wrestler names would be.

"Watch this!" Doc said.

Abby looked down at her notebook. Her mom had married Doc's dad three years before, so she was used to him. They mostly got along. But sometimes she felt it was best to ignore him.

For example, any time he said "Watch this!"

"I'm really gonna do it," he said.

"I'm trying to read," she said.

"Here goes!" he said.

"Hold on!" a voice shouted. "Don't jump on me!"

Doc looked at Abby.

"That wasn't me," she said.

"Don't jump!" the voice said again. A man's voice.

Abby pointed to the big box. "Almost sounds like it was coming from . . ."

The box shook. Something was moving around inside it.

The voice said, "It's so dark in here." The box flaps flipped

open, and the voice said, "Ah, that's better."

Then a black hat appeared, then a head, then a chest. It was a tall man in a black suit. He had a thin, bony face and wild hair sticking out from under his hat.

He looked a lot like Abraham Lincoln.

STEVE SHEINKIN used to write textbooks, and he's very sorry about that. But now he writes good books, like *Undefeated, Most Dangerous, The Port Chicago 50, Bomb,* and *The Notorious Benedict Arnold*. He's a three-time National Book Award Finalist and has won a Newbery Honor. Steve lives with his family in Saratoga Springs, New York. **stevesheinkin.com**